DIAL AND DRIVEN TO DARKNESS

SHUBHAM KATARIYA

Made with ♥ on the Notion Press Platform
www.notionpress.com

To my incredible parents, Neeraj Kumar and Poonam,

Your love has been the guiding light of my life, illuminating even the darkest paths with warmth and hope. Your unwavering support, gentle encouragement, and profound wisdom have been my pillars of strength, allowing me to dream without limits and persevere without fear.

You have taught me the value of kindness, the power of resilience, and the importance of staying true to myself. This book is not just a result of my efforts but a reflection of the values, love, and lessons you've instilled in me.

Thank you for believing in me even when I doubted myself, for cheering me on in every endeavor, and for shaping the person I am today.

This is for you, with all my love and deepest gratitude.

Contents

Contents

About The Author

" A decent boy who is a magician of words "

Shubham Katariya is a passionate writer who loves to read and craft stories that captivate the imagination. With a deep love for the written word, Shubham has honed his skills in writing not only books but also poetry, quotes, and articles. His ability to weave emotions, suspense, and deep insights into his writing allows him to explore various genres and express his creative visions.

How To Read A Book

I have written these stories chapter wise so that it becomes easier for you to read. There are two stories in the book, both are horror, first read the first story and then read the second one.

Foreword

In our increasingly modern world, stories that chill us to the core serve as a stark reminder of the mysteries lurking just beyond the edges of what we understand. The Cursed Phone and Driven to Darkness are not just tales of horror and suspense; they are explorations of the human psyche when confronted with the unknown.

Shubham Katariya masterfully blends fear, emotion, and suspense in a way that keeps readers on the edge of their seats. Through his vivid storytelling, he examines the fragility of trust, the consequences of unchecked curiosity, and the resilience of the human spirit when faced with unimaginable terror.

These stories are more than mere entertainment—they are thought-provoking journeys into the fears that bind us and the courage that defines us. As you embark on these adventures, prepare for unexpected twists, relentless suspense, and haunting revelations.

Shubham has crafted a compelling collection that not only captivates but also challenges us to question how we confront the darkness within and around us. This book is an invitation to explore the boundaries of courage, fear, and the unknown.

Preface

In a world where curiosity often collides with fear, Driven to Darkness and The Cursed Phone unravel tales of humanity's struggle against forces beyond comprehension. These stories delve into the fragility of trust, the weight of betrayal, and the unrelenting grip of the unknown.

Through haunting twists and chilling revelations, they explore the boundaries between light and shadow, pushing characters to confront their deepest fears and darkest choices. Both tales serve as a stark reminder: some mysteries are better left unsolved, and some paths lead only to darkness.

Step into these worlds, but tread carefully—for once you enter, there may be no escape.

Acknowledgements

Writing this book has been a journey of imagination, inspiration, and reflection, and it would not have been possible without the support and guidance of many incredible people.First and foremost, I thank my parents, for their endless love, encouragement, and belief in my dreams. To my friend himani, Your support has been my greatest strength. thank you for standing by me during the late nights and long days, offering your encouragement and insights. Your faith in me kept my passion alive. Lastly, I am grateful to everyone who has ever dared to step into the unknown and confront their fears. This book is a tribute to your courage. Thank you for being part of this journey.

Prologue

In The Cursed Phone, a mysterious device falls into the hands of six unsuspecting friends. What begins as an object of curiosity soon reveals its dark intent—haunting them with whispers of their fears and uncovering secrets meant to stay buried. As the curse tightens its grip, they realize the price of survival might be more than they're willing to pay.

In Driven to Darkness, betrayal and desperation lead a family down a harrowing path where trust is shattered, and evil festers in the most unexpected places. Shadows of the past collide with the present, leaving no one untouched by the chilling truths they must confront.

Both stories are tales of fear, sacrifice, and the unrelenting pull of the unknown, where survival demands the ultimate test of courage.

1 - story

The cursed phone

Characters:

Aryan - An inquisitive and well informed person whose interest with secrets and rush leads him to keep the reviled telephone.

Pallavi - Aryan's down to earth and careful sweetheart, who has major areas of strength for an of endurance.

Kabir - Aryan's lifelong companion who's bold, thrill-chasing, and frequently careless, able to push limits.

Sonali - Touchy and profoundly adjusted, she feels the vindictive presence right away and urges alert.

Harshita - Brave and intrepid, she's generally quick to confront risk yet is profoundly offbeat.

Tushar - The normal, distrustful companion who demands tracking down legitimate clarifications in spite of the spooky events around them.

1

The Mysterious Find

On a stormy evening, Aryan finds an old, dust-free phone lying on an otherwise dirty train seat. When he was coming back from coaching. It was the strangest phone he had ever seen. He picked up the phone and looked at it. The phone's screen flickers between static and the image of a shadowy figure, though no one seems to be nearby. A strange chill washes over him as he picked it up. He thought this phone's battery was down. He kept the phone in his bag. Unknowingly sealing the fate of his friends and himself in ways he could never have imagined.

2

Ominous Messages

Aryan reached home, freshened up, had dinner and then went to his room. Then he studied for a while and then he remembered about the phone which he had met in the train. He took out the phone from the bag and started examining it. It was a dark night outside, dogs were barking and it was also cold. He examined the phone closely. Suddenly, the screen lights up, and chilling messages appear: "I'm watching you." As Aryan stareds in shock, the background changes, showing a distorted figure with hollow eyes. More messages reveal details about Aryan's past and secrets only he knows only. He got scared and threw the phone on the bed and asked in a scared voice, "Who are you?" Whose phone is this? The phone did not respond and then he went near the phone. He picked up the phone again in his hand and started looking inside the phone. Then a strange ring ringed on the phone and a message came. The phone's final message freezes him: "Welcome to your end, Aryan." he is scared and went to sleep with his mother.

3

The Haunting Call

The next day, Aryan went to his college and called his friends home. He gathered his friends to show them the strange messages, thinking it's a harmless mystery. After hearing all this, Aryan's friends laughed at him. They feel that he has seen some strange dream. But Aryan is scared and remembers whatever happened to him at night. Suddenly the phone ringed Aryan hesitates, then answers. A chilling whisper on the other end murmurs, "I'm watching all of you." They dismiss it was a prank call, but Sonali felt a dark, cold presence in the room, sensing something sinister has entered their lives. Everyone found it was a prank and everyone went home while laughing. She started believing Aryan's words to be true.

4

The Dark History

Kabir went to his home and thought about the phone, he liked doing research and he sat down to do research on the phone. He searched online for cursed phone stories and found accounts of a similar device associated with mysterious deaths. He got a heart-wrenching discovery about his phone. Kabir's hands start trembling. Each victim had been tormented by visions and eerie incidents before dying in horrific ways. And he got scared and called aryan and told him the whole truth about the phone. But Aryan's curiosity grows stronger, feeling an odd, hypnotic pull toward the device.

5
Shocking Dreams

Aryan had started feeling troubled ever since that phone had come into his life. Nor did he talk to his friends. He used to just lay in his room His family and all his friends started worrying about him. He had also reduced coming to college. One day Pallavi went to his house to ask about everything.

Then what she came to know, Pallavi started crying while hugging him. He started having vivid, disturbing dreams where he sees shadowy figures clawing toward him and glimpses of his own death. Then she told that thing to his friends and everyone was surprised. Next morning, aryan found a series of photos on the cursed phone, taken while he was sleeping. The last photo is inches from his face, showing a pair of ghostly eyes staring back at him from beside his bed. He started sweating and screamed in fear. Shaken, He tried to delete the photos, but they reappear moments later, with each image more terrifying than the last. He cried............

6

The Primary Exchange

Aryan told Pallavi everything that happened to him this morning in college. Then she calms him down and says I will come to your house at night and then let's do something with that phone. She came to his house that night and she picked up the phone to throw it away. The screen lights up, showing a picture of her from moments before, as if taken by an invisible hand. She's scared yet attempts to get over it as an error. Unbeknownst to her, this basic activity moves the revile consideration regarding her, setting off a chain of lethal results.

7

Harshita's Oddity Mishap

Pallavi told everything to Harshita, she found it all a joke. She felt that everything was nonsense, these people were unnecessarily scared. Harshita known for her thrill-seeking, she went to Aryan's house to take the phone from him. She took the phone from Aryan and got back to her home with the phone and kept the phone on her table. Then after 1 hour phone ringed she got up and looked at the phone. The screen shows a chilling image of her face twisted in terror, with the words: "You're next." She laughed and thought it was a joke, she slept. Next morning she narrowly survives a horrific car accident, but the experienced left her shaken. She started seeing eerie shadowy figures that follow her everywhere, whispering her name and creeping closer each day then that voice started bothering her becoming darker and more menacing.

8

Counseling the Medium

Then the whole group planned to meet a medium (paranormal expert) and find out about the phone. Then they came to know that there is a woman living behind the river in the city who tells them all these things. They all reached that aunty. Then Pallavi told the whole thing to aunty and aunty asked Harshita for that phone. She gave phone to that aunty and she shudders upon touching the phone and warns them. Aunty said nervously it's bound by a curse—one of vengeance and relentless hatred. She revealed that the spirit in the phone is a tormented soul, cursed to seek eternal revenge. Hearing this whole group got scared and they all got worried. Aryan asked aunty, how can we all save ourselves from this? She told them that someone died in terrible agony, binding their soul to the phone. The only way to escape is to transfer the curse or destroy the phone, though it might cost them dearly. Pallavi said aunty there can't be any other treatment, what is it aunty said no children. Everyone returned home disappointed and scared.

9

A Dark Decision

Pallavi invited everyone to come to her house for next pan about the phone. Everyone reached Pallavi's place on time. Then the whole group discussed and nothing is answered for 2 hours. Everyone sat down dejectedly and looked at each other, then tushar suggested finding a stranger to pass the curse on to, but Sonali is horrified at the thought of hurting an innocent person. Half group with him and half with her. A fight broke out among the group and everyone started shouting at each other. The friends are divided, and their trust began to break under the strain. The phone ringed and the message is displayed on the phone "hahahah idiots" As paranoia grows, the phone starts to reveal their deepest fears and secrets, widening the rift between them and stoking feelings of betrayal.

10

The Spirit's anger

all the people have decided that they will always keep the phone with them, so Kabir keeps it with himself first.He left the phone at home and went off to complete his work and came back at night and went to sleep. Nothing happened to him on the first day. Next morninghe got fever and did not go to college and stayed at home. He heard his name being called outside his window. Turning around, he found his own distorted face staring back at him from the phone screen. He thought he was feeling like he has a fever and ignored it that night, he heard his name being called outside his window again. From that point on, he felt the presence of an unseen force, moving objects in his room, scratching at his window, and leaving dark marks on his walls. He began to spiral into madness, driven by fear and sleepless nights. He called all his friends to his house and told everything. The phone's grip tightens, and each friend began to see visions of their own death. Tushar tried to film the phone to gather evidence, but in the video, he saw himself decayed and lifeless, mouthing words he can't understand. Utterly shocked, he began to accept that this curse goes beyond rationality or science.

11

Ritual for Salvation

Pallavi desperately searched for a book. She got the book and takes it with her, reached Aryan's home. Pallavi told Aryan that there is a method to escape from the curse. He became happy after hearing this, desperate bid to rid them of the curse, attempt an ancient ritual they found in a forbidden occult text. First they made a circle with sandalwood powder and placed the phone in the middle. Then they light 6 candles and switched off the lights of the room. They started chanting mantras to vanish the curse of the phone. The ritual seems to work, but as they finished, the phone screen displays a chilling image of Sonali's face, bloodied and hollow-eyed. A new message appears: "Too late." They realized the spirit has grown stronger and even more wrathful.

12

Shadow of Despair

The curse reached a peak, and each of them is haunted by their impending doom. Everyone started feeling that they would not survive. Everyone was crying in their homes and could not even tell anyone else. It seemed as if the end of everything was certain now. Pallavi dreams of drowning in a dark, bottomless lake; tushar sees himself engulfed in flames; Sonali hears chilling voices whispering "The end is near" wherever she goes, and Aryan feels an icy, skeletal grip tugging at him constantly. Each passing day, their lives become a living nightmare, consumed by fear and darkness. One day Sonali got upset with all this and went to the train where Aryan found the phone. She went and said you are here; tell me what else you want. There, she experienced a vision of the spirit's past: a woman who was betrayed by those closest to her, left to die in a pitiless rage. Before dying, she cursed them all, binding her soul to the phone to seek vengeance. She realized the spirit's hunger for revenge will never be satisfied; it feeds on their suffering and will continue to torment them until it has consumed everyone connected to the phone.

13

The Last Stand

Sonali called all the friends of her and said we have to apologize to this soul. I hope she may leave us after this. Armed with this revelation, the friends confronted the spirit together, apologizing and pleading for release. But the spirit only laughed, showing them terrifying images of their mangled, lifeless bodies on the phone screen. Now everyone knows that they are going to die, the spirit will not leave them. They realized that their only option is to destroy the phone, but doing so may mean risking their own lives. The gathering turned on one another in their urgency to get by. Tushar covertly attempted to pass the telephone to an outsider, expecting to get away from the revile, yet Aryan got him in the demonstration. An actual quarrel breaks out as trust falls, with every one of them expecting that the other will forfeit them. The soul revels in their division, blossoming with their trepidation and question. One evening, pallavi narrowly escaped a near-fatal accident after receiving a message from the phone warning her of her impending death. She realized that the spirit's power extends beyond the phone, manipulating reality to fulfill its dark agenda. With no options left, she begged Aryan to end the curse at any cost.

"Silence the phone, but you can't silence the screams."

14

one twist and one scarify

Sonali truly loved Aryan but only she knew this. And she did not tell this to anyone else because he was already in a relationship. Aryan called his friends and said that this has started because of me and I will end it too. Sonali got scared after hearing this; she did not want anything to happen to Aryan. And after hearing this, she went to Aryan's house. He was sleeping. Sonali, that cursed phone, got up from the table and said in a low voice, I love you Aryan, I will not let anything happen to you. There was a field outside Aryan's house; she had gone to that field. In a final act of courage, Sonali offered herself as a sacrifice, holding the phone and pleading with the spirit to release her friends. As she spoke, the spirit consumes her, leaving her lifeless body behind while the phone shatters to the ground. The others look on in horror, praying that her sacrifice has finally broken the curse. Next morning, when all the friends come to know about all this, they got very upset. But somewhere it was also believed that they had got freedom from that cursed phone.

"You can destroy the phone, but not the curse it carries."

15

The Last Bend

After Sonali's tragic sacrificed, the friends tried to move forward, haunted but relieved. Yet small, unsettling signs appear—strange shadows, whispers in the dark, unexplained chills in empty rooms. It dawns on them that while the spirit's rage has been temporarily quelled, it hasn't truly left them. Just as they started to believe they're free, Aryan's new phone buzzes with a familiar ringtone. His blood runs cold as he saw a message on the screen: "You can't escape me." In horror, he realized the curse has merely transferred to a new device. The story closed on a scream, hinting that their nightmare is far from over.

Thus, "the cursed phone remains a haunting reminder that some spirits never rest".

story - 2

Driven to Darkness

16

The Bargain

Yash needed a new car but had a tight budget. He went to auction then he saw an old, sleek black SUV for sale at an unbelievable price, he couldn't resist. The seller was eager to part with it, avoiding Yash's questions about its history. As Yash drove it home, he felt a slight chill, happy dismissing it as excitement. He named the car *queenie,* not knowing it had a sinister past. He drank too much at night and fell asleep.

17

Strange Occurrences

The next day Yash took his car to the mountain and came back at night, then he noticed

Strange things—the radio turned on by itself, playing static or old songs he'd never heard. The car locks clicked and clacked unpredictably, and the headlights flickered at random, the sunroof of the car was open and closed again and again. Jack tried to rationalize it as electrical issues, but the discomfort gnawed at him. But he couldn't shake the feeling that queenie was... aware......

18

The Hitchhiker

Yash has returned from his office One foggy night,yash saw a figure by the roadside. He slowed down, but before he could fully stop, queenie seemed to accelerate by itself. The figure's eyes locked with Yash's, filled with terror. yash pulled over, but the figure was gone. The next day, he noticed a handprint smeared on the passenger window, a reminder of someone unseen he got shocked after noticed this paranormal activity his car has done with him last night.

19

The First Warning

One day yash was cleaning his car and found an old cassette under the driver's seat.he was very curious, he played it, hearing only static at first, but then a faint voice broke through: *"Run before its too late." I will kill you* ".Startled, he ejected it, but the cassette reappeared every time he checked the car. It felt like a warning from someone who once sat where he now sat. he got scared and trying to know about car history.

20

The Darkness Inside

As days passed, yash felt increasingly uneasy in the car. *queenie* would sometimes lock him inside, trapping him in a dark, pindrop silence. Strange scratches appeared on the windows, forming words he couldn't quite make out. One night, in the rearview mirror, he saw a face staring back at him—a shadowy figure with hollow eyes, seated in the back seat. "*Run before it's too late*" was written repeatedly on the windshield of his car. His car horn used to sound again and again.

21

The Mechanic's Fear

Desperate, yash took queenie to a mechanic. The man seemed disturbed upon inspecting it and refused to work on it, muttering, "Some things are best left alone." Before yash left, the mechanic whispered, *"Get rid of it, son. Some cars carry more than just passengers."* yash laughed nervously, but the fear lingered. Yash was very scared and took his car towards his home and started thinking about the history of the car.

22

History Revealed

Determined to uncover the car's past, yash researched online and discovered a chilling history. *queenie* had belonged to a man named Charles, who mysteriously vanished after driving it. A few others had owned it since, each experiencing strange events,something very paranormal, some leading to accidents, and all owners eventually abandoned or sold it under equally strange circumstances. yash began to realize the car was a dark magnet for tragedy.

23

Voices in the Night

One night, as yash drove home late, whispers filled the car, calling his name, begging for help. He gripped the steering wheel tightly, trying to ignore them, but the voices grew louder, echoing through his mind. He saw shadowy figures at the edge of his vision, their hands reaching for him. Panicked, he tried to stop the car, but the brakes wouldn't respond. Yash escapes from an accident or the car stopped, he gets worried about the car or finds out about its owners, then he finds out about an owner who lives in a forest far away from the city. Yash leaves for the owner's house the next morning.

24

yash reached to destination

Yash reached her house and ringed the doorbell. Buddhi Amma (old woman) opened the gate and asked himto come inside. Yash went inside her house and fearfully told about the car. she got scared after hearing this and said history is repeating. She spoke of her own experience with queenie and the horrific accident that claimed her son's life while they were in it. She believed the car held the spirit of someone vengeful, trapping each owner in a spiral of misfortune. Her advice was chilling: "Abandon it, or it'll claim you too." Yash didn't believe on her story and said it's nothing like that; she's a liar and left her home

25

Yash's decision

Yash came back his home and went to sleep in his room but him unabled to sleep. The thoughts of that period were running through his mind. Yash got worried and wonders what to do now. Yash woke up from bed, washed his face and says in the mirror, now I will not drive this car anymore, I will break it. Then a voice came to his ears. *"You'll never be rid of me."* Yash decided to drive *queenie* to the edge of town and leave it, but the car seemed to resist, veering off the road and forcing him back. The voices grew louder, filling his mind with images of fire, darkness, and screaming faces.Yash fought for control, but queenie had its own destination in mind Realizing he could not escape, Yash confronted the car, shouting at it to reveal what it wanted. Suddenly, the car went silent, and the radio crackled to life. A voice, low and menacing, spoke: *"You'll never be rid of me."* yash understood that the car wasn't just haunted—it was alive, feeding on his fear and despair.

26

The Next morning

The next morning, yash was found unconscious by the roadside. His car had crashed, but there were no signs of impact. Shaken, he realized he had no memory of the crash. When he approached *queenie* to assess the damage, he saw his own name scratched into the paint, like a final warning. He left his car on the road and went to his home he was very scared of car, he fainted on the floor. After few hours, Yash noticed the strange events weren't limited to the car anymore. He heard *queenie's* engine revving outside his window at night, saw its headlights flickering. He tried hiding the keys, but they always reappeared on his pocket. The car was everywhere he went, even when he wasn't in it. Yash realized he could never escape. *queenie* was bound to him now, a curse he'd have to carry for life.

27

A Friend's come

Yash called his best friend; his name was Shubham and asked him to come home. he got ready to come home and reached Yash's house that night. As soon as he saw him, he hugged him and started crying. And he kept saying, save me brother. Then he told the whole story to him. He told him that we will have to go back to that woman and ask her in detail what happened to her and her son. Yash hugged Shubham and started crying and shouted, do something quickly.

28

The mystery story

Yash and Shubham reached that woman's house the next day.They started asking that woman, tell us grandma, what happened to you, and tell us the story. We want to know about that. Grandma started crying and started telling them the story. He told us that 15 years have passed since her and his son were going to the city suddenly the brakes of the car failed and the car hit the tree or his son died at his accident. Then the police came, the ambulance came, it did not seem like the car had an accident because there was no scratch on the car. I understood that this was done by some evil force which was on the car. Then we sold that car and are living in a forest away from the city. Then Shubham asked grandma how we can avoid this. Grandma said son, you also sell this car to someone else and avoid these things. Then he said that we cannot leave like this, we cannot put anyone else's life in trouble, because in last 15 years we have lost the lives of many people, we have to get permanent treatment. Grandma said, Beta, there is a lot of danger in this don't be stubborn, sell it. Then Yash said, Grandma, we are ready to take the risk, can you show us the way? Then grandmother said okay, I will tell you.

29

The new hope

Then grandmother took us to a paranormal expert in the middle of the forest and said, "My work has done; now you both see." What to do.

The name of paranormal expert is Om Prakash. He asked us to sit and said, tell me what the problem is. We sat down and heard strange sounds all around us as if there were some kind of animals. Candles were burning all around his house And Om Prakash looked at us and said tell me children, how did you come here? Then I told the whole thing to the expert and he told us that he will fix everything, please give him 1 hours' time. We were happy to hear from him and started waiting for him for 1 hour. Then he started doing high work and sent us to another room and told us not to come here until I call you. An hour had passed, he called us to his room, we saw that he had kept a mirror and there was a black smoke in it. He says that there is a girl's soul in your car, something bad has happened to her that is why she is taking revenge, she has not killed Yash yet because he wanted to know about her past and help her. Both of you will have to come on the day of New Moon, on that day I will call her spirit and she will tell you everything

30

New moon day

We both reached on the day of New Moon and saw that expert was waiting for us. He told us to sit and hold this stick in your hands. Then he explained to us that there is nothing to be afraid of, he will take care of everything. Shubham and I were scared. Then the expert placed his mirror in front of us and started calling her. he started drawing something on the mirror with his finger and there was a ring on his finger which was glowing. And then a strange sound started coming from the mirror.

31

The entity arrival

Gradually the voice became louder and black smoke started coming from the mirror. The expert told us that she is coming. We closed our eyes after seeing a bright light coming from the mirror and as soon as we opened our eyes we saw a girl flying in the air. Her hair was open, her clothes were torn from her hands, and there were blood marks on her face and body. The expert told us that now you both can ask about her past.

Then she started telling about her past, when she was 17 years old she fell in love a boy named Rohit .she loved him wholeheartedly and there was no one who can separate them . They used to go on dates, walking together hand in hand and many more. Like this they created a lot of memories together. But she was so busy in her beautiful life that she forgot the most important thing about her, that she belonged to a very poor family whereas Rohit was from a very rich family. But she was so busy spending the beautiful moments of her life that she didn't pay much attention to it and thought everything's gonna be alright.

32

The truth

Then one day Rohit called me and took me on a date and made me sit in the car with my seat belt on. We got into the car, suddenly Rohit said now I don't want you i love somebody else and gives a strange smile and speeds up the car. The road was about to end and I was shouting to Rohit, stop the car. he did not stop the car and jumped out from the car, i got stuck in the seat belt and the car exploded and I could not escape. Then after a few days a car dealer repaired the car by repainting the dent or sold the car then I started taking revenge from everyone who drives this car because they couldn't help me and I didn't trust anyone anymore. Then one day Yash bought a car and he wanted to help me. That's why I didn't kill Yash. Now Yash is the owner of that car and only Yash can help me.

33

The plan

I asked that spirit how will Yash help you? She told that I want to kill Rohit but I cannot touch him, he has protected himself from me with some magical spell. I need Yash's body for some time so that I can kill Rohit, nothing will happen to Yash. After listening, he and I looked at each other, after thinking a little, He said yes. She smiled and said be ready for tomorrow meet me at yash's house on 8 PM with the car. Then we thanked the paranormal expert and went towards home.

34

The final toll

It was about to be 8 o'clock and yash and i were waiting for her. As soon as 8 o'clock she came in front of us and entered Yash's body. Yash's voice changed and I got scared after seeing the way he walked too. Then she started the car and started taking the car to the place where Rohit had murdered her. Then Rohit's car is seen on the way and she overtakes his car and stopped it.

Rohit came from the car and said who are you, what

happened? She also came out from the car and spoke "remember me rohit " hahaha I am back to meet you my love he acknowledges her voice and said twinkle are u still alive you can't do anything to me hahaha I will kill you again. Meanwhile, that spirit got angry and hits Rohit on the face. He wonders how she touched me and got scared and sat in his car. Trying to start the car, the car didn't start. Then she tied Rohit's seat belt in the car seat and he was not able to open the seat belt. Then that soul came from Yash's body and gave a creepy smile to him. Then that soul entered Yash's body again and pushed the car off the cliff and the car explodes. Rohit got killed and it gets expelled from Yash's body or it disappeared.

Author's Note

Thank you very much to all of you for reading my book.

I would love to hear your feedback, thoughts, and ideas! Connect with me via email or on social media to share your experience with this book or discuss what you'd like to see next.

Thank you for reading,

Shubham Katariya

shubhikatariya56@gmail.com

www.ingramcontent.com/pod-product-compliance
Lightning Source LLC
La Vergne TN
LVHW041130150826
845673LV00007B/2254

* 9 7 9 8 8 9 6 3 2 1 8 4 2 *